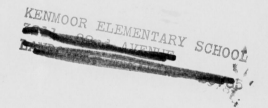

The Cellar

Books by
Ellen Howard

Circle of Giving
When Daylight Comes
Gillyflower
Edith Herself
Her Own Song
Sister
The Chickenhouse House
The Cellar

THE CELLAR

by *Ellen Howard*

illustrated by
Patricia Mulvihill

A JEAN KARL BOOK

Atheneum   1992   New York

Maxwell Macmillan Canada   *Toronto*
Maxwell Macmillan International
Publishing Group
New York   Oxford   Singapore   Sydney

Atheneum
Macmillan Publishing Company
866 Third Avenue
New York, NY 10022
Maxwell Macmillan Canada, Inc.
1200 Eglinton Avenue East
Suite 200
Don Mills, Ontario M3C 3N1
*Macmillan Publishing Company is part of the
Maxwell Communication Group of Companies.*

First edition
Printed in the United States of America
10 9 8 7 6 5 4 3 2 1
The text of this book is set in 14 pt. Century Book.
The illustrations are rendered in pencil.
Book design by Kimberly M. Adlerman

Library of Congress Cataloging-in-Publication Data

Howard, Ellen.
*The cellar / by Ellen Howard: illustrated by
Patricia Mulvihill.*
p.   cm.
"A Jean Karl book."
*Summary: Even though her brothers
tease her about not being big
enough to do any of the important jobs
on the farm, Faith proves
that she is brave enough to go down into
the dark cellar for apples.*
ISBN 0–689–31724–7
*[1. Farm life—Fiction.   2. Brothers and sisters—
Fiction.]*
I. Mulvihill, Patricia, ill.   II. Title.
PZ7.H83274Ce   1991
[Fic]—dc20   90-23190

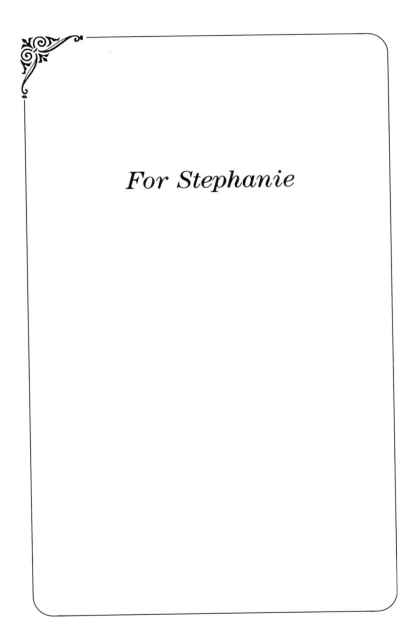

For Stephanie

Our Father's Big Cellar

How well I remember the old home's big cellar. Its hard floor of earth, the cool walls of white stone ... (and) a big slanting doorway where we children could slide.

> —From the "Memory Book"
> of Ruth Ellen Rohrbough
> Weger Dunkelberger,
> written in 1970 when she
> was ninety years old

When the evening chores were finished
And the supper time was o'er,
We'd watch the blazes flicker
Through the mica on the door
Of that faithful round oak heater
That so many years we use'
To gather round in evening time
While Father read the news.

Oft' time the question would arise
And was often argued o'er
Who would bring those juicy apples
Up from out the winter's store.
Those grand old luscious apples ...

> —From "Memories," by
> Stephen Strange
> Rohrbough, written in 1932

Contents

1
Morning

"Here, biddy-biddy, chick-chick-chick!" called Faith.

She reached into her bucket for a handful of corn. She watched it fly from her fingers in a spray of gold.

The hens crowded out of the chickenhouse. They made an eager clucking as they fluttered and flapped.

"Here, biddy-biddy, chick-chick-chick!" Faith called again.

Faith scattered another handful of corn.

Peck, peck, peck.

There was a pain in Faith's big toe.

"Ow!" she cried, looking down.

The old Plymouth Rock hen was pecking her boot.

"Greedy!" said Faith, shaking her foot.

She dumped a handful of corn on the Plymouth Rock's head.

The hen squawked and gave her a startled glance. Then peck, peck, peck. She gobbled the grain on the hard, packed ground, unaware of the corn on her featherless head.

"Ready or not, here I come!"

Faith heard Fritz yell from the side of the house.

"Whoa, boy, not so fast," came William's voice. He was laughing hard.

Her brothers were playing while she was obliged to do chores, Faith thought.

Faith glanced toward the kitchen door. Mother was nowhere in sight. Faith upended her bucket.

"Scatter the grain evenly," Mother always said. "If the corn isn't scattered, the hens will squabble."

That was what had happened to the Plymouth Rock's head. When she snatched feed away from the other hens, they had pecked her bald.

Faith kicked at the mound of

corn she had dumped on the ground. It would be all right this once, she thought. Scattering took too long!

She hurried around the side of the house, toward her brothers' voices. Behind her she could hear the hens squawking.

William and Fritz were sliding on feed sacks on the cellar door, which sloped steeply against the side of the house.

"Yahoo!" yelled William as he hurtled down its slope. He landed in a laughing heap.

"Hey," called Faith. "May I play too?"

She began to run.

Fritz was climbing up the cellar door. He turned his head when he heard Faith call.

THE CELLAR

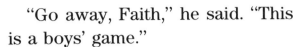

"Go away, Faith," he said. "This is a boys' game."

"Why?" said Faith. She was panting from her run. Her face felt hot and sweaty, despite the cool fall morning. "Why can't I play?" she said.

"The cellar door is steep," Fritz said. "You'll get scared, or you'll hurt yourself."

"No, I won't," said Faith. "I won't get scared, and I won't get hurt. I can do it."

"Oh, let her try," said William. "What's the harm?"

"This is a boys' game," said Fritz. His face looked sulky. But William was the oldest. Fritz usually did what his brother said.

"I can do it," said Faith. She began to climb onto the cellar door.

"No fair helping her," Fritz told William, who had put out his hand to steady her. "Wait your turn, Faith. It's *my* turn now."

Faith climbed back off and waited.

Fritz scrambled on up the cellar door. He dropped his feed sack and stood on it.

"Watch! Standing up!" he cried.

He pushed off from the house.

"Yahoo!" he yelled and slid down, standing up.

It looked like great fun to Faith.

"Now, *my* turn," she said, grabbing the sack.

Faith began to climb up the cellar door. It was hard to climb and hold on to the sack at the same time. She dropped to her knees and crawled. First one hand and knee forward, then the other, dragging the sack, up went Faith.

Faith was at the top. She was breathing hard. She turned around and sat on the sack. It felt slippery beneath her. She saw Fritz and William watching her. The ground seemed a long way down.

Faith could feel her smile fading. She tried to keep the corners of her mouth bravely turned up. She imagined how it would feel to slide fast down the door. To slide fast. . . . Too fast?

"Slide," said Fritz. "Slide!"

"Take your time, Faithie," William said. "If you feel afraid, I'll help you down."

"Yah, Baby Faith," Fritz said, "we'll help you down if you're *scared.*"

"I'm not scared," said Faith. But her voice was quivery. Her hands held on hard to the top of the door.

"Then slide!" said Fritz.

Faith took a deep breath. She closed her eyes. She lifted her legs. But her hands would not let go.

Faith lowered her legs and opened her eyes.

"Do you want me to help you?" William said.

Faith shook her head hard.

"Then slide!" said Fritz.

Faith shook her head.

"Come *on,*" Fritz said. "It's William's turn."

"I don't care about my turn," said William.

"Faith-*ie!*" said Fritz.

"Let me help you," said William.

Faith shook her head.

"I can do it," she said.

"William! Fritz!" It was Father's voice, coming from the barn.

William reached up to Faith. "Just grab my hand," he said.

"No," said Faith, turning away her head. Her heart was beating, *thump, thump, thump!*

"William! Fritz!"

"We have to go, Faith," William said, his voice worried. "Father's calling."

Faith shook her head.

"Well, *I'm* not going to get in trouble while *she* makes up her mind," said Fritz. "*I'm* going."

Faith heard his footsteps running across the yard.

She could feel William looking at her.

"I can do it," she said.

William backed away. Faith could feel him getting farther from her.

"Just holler if you need me to help you down," he said.

Faith nodded her head a little nod. She felt the feed sack slip beneath her. She held on more tightly to the top of the door.

"William," she said in a tiny voice.

But William's footsteps were running too, away toward the barn.

Faith turned her head and watched him until he ran through the barn door.

Her arms were aching from holding on. Her feet were scrabbling for

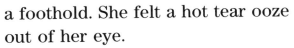

a foothold. She felt a hot tear ooze out of her eye.

Slowly Faith turned over, the feed sack slippery beneath her. She felt with her feet for a way to climb down. Her hands loosened their grip.

Then whoosh went the air past Faith's face. Her hair lifted. Her skirts flew up. As she slid on her stomach down the door, she heard her stocking rip.

"Ow!" cried Faith. Thump! Crash!

Faith found herself sitting on the ground. Her knee was hurting. The feed sack was over her head. Her face was wet with crying.

2
Afternoon

"I notice," said Mother as she washed Faith's hurt knee, "that the Plymouth Rock's head is bleeding too. Are you sure you took time to *scatter* the corn?"

Faith hung her head.

"Oh, Faithie," Mother said.

She tied a bandage around Faith's leg. She picked up Faith's torn stocking and clucked her tongue.

"Put this in the mending bag," she said. "Then put on clean stockings. Alena will help you to button your boots."

Faith crept out of the kitchen, not able to look at Mother's face.

"Faith," said Mother, "please find something *quiet* to do until dinner."

By dinnertime Faith was feeling better. *This* afternoon she would stay out of trouble, she told herself. She would be a big girl and a help.

Big sister Alena went to sit on the porch after dinner. She was hemming towels for Mother.

"May I hem a towel for you?" Faith said.

"You may stitch on your sampler," said Mother.

So Faith found her embroidery

sampler. She went to sit on the porch.

Faith put her needle through the cloth that was stretched on her embroidery frame. She tried to put it through one of the marks Mother had made to guide her. The needle went *almost* right. She poked at the back of the cloth with the needle, trying to find the place to pull it out again. There, that was it. That was *almost* it.

Faith put her head to one side and studied the stitch. It was too big and crooked. Perhaps Mother wouldn't notice. She smoothed it with her finger. Now there was a smudge on the cloth. How could her fingers be dirty so soon? She had washed them just before dinner.

THE CELLAR

Faith sighed. She kicked her feet against the chair rung. She bounced on her bottom a little.

"Are you cold, Faithie, sitting out here?" Alena said. "I think the wind is coming up. It's chilly without a shawl."

"*I'll* fetch your shawl if you want," said Faith.

She jumped up, and her sampler fell off her lap. It landed in the dirt at the foot of the steps.

"Oh, Faithie!" Alena said. "*Do* take care. Now look what you've done."

Faith snatched up her sampler. She shook off the dust. She put it behind her back.

"It isn't harmed," she said. "Do you want your shawl, Alena?"

Alena shivered and rubbed her arms.

"Yes, yes," she said. "Go fetch our shawls. I can see you're as fidgety as a cat with fleas."

Faith ran upstairs.

Alena's brown wool shawl was neatly folded on the chest, but Faith couldn't find her own. She looked in her drawer. She looked on the chair. She looked on the hooks behind the door. Finally she saw a bit of blue fringe peeking from under the bed.

"How did you get there?" she said to her shawl as she pulled it out.

When Faith came downstairs, Alena had come into the kitchen.

"Thank you, Faithie," she said. "I don't need my shawl now. I'm helping Mother. Just put it on the hook."

"May I help?" Faith said.

"You can help by finishing that row of stitches on your sampler," Mother said.

"I'm tired of stitching," said Faith.

"Just one row," said Mother.

"I could help you," said Faith.

"*Just one row*," said Mother.

Faith sighed and stomped outdoors. She tied on her shawl before she sat down. Alena was right. The wind *was* coming up.

Fritz and William walked by the porch.

"Where are you going?" called Faith.

"None of your business, Baby Faith," said Fritz.

"To bring in the cows," said William.

"May I come too?" said Faith.

"Bringing in the cows is boys' work," said Fritz.

"I could help," said Faith.

"It's too far for a little girl to go," said Fritz. "You'll get tired."

"No, I won't," said Faith. "I won't get tired."

"Oh, let her come," said William.

Fritz looked disgusted.

"I'm going with the boys to bring in the cows," Faith called through the screened door to Mother. She ran down the steps before Mother could answer.

"Walk behind us," said Fritz.

Faith walked behind William and Fritz. They walked through the barnyard and down the path.

"I'm not too young to go after the

cows," Faith said. "I'm not getting tired."

Fritz kicked at the grass with his bare foot. He switched at the bushes with his willow switch. He looked over his shoulder at Faith.

" 'Course, *you're* wearing boots," he said. "Only *boys* go barefoot so late in the fall."

"I can go barefoot," said Faith.

"Don't pay any mind to Fritz," said William. "You don't have to go barefoot. The ground is cold, and the stones are sharp, and there are stickers in the grass."

"They won't hurt me," said Faith.

Faith sat down in the middle of the path. She struggled with the buttons on her boots. Her breath came hard in little gasps. She felt her face get hot.

The boys were far ahead.

"Wait for me," called Faith.

"Don't take off your boots," William said.

"Come on, Baby Faith," said Fritz.

Faith pulled off one boot. She pulled off the other. She pulled off her clean stockings.

"Wait for me," called Faith.

"Hurry," said William. "It's milking time. Father is waiting for the cows."

"Hurry, Baby Faith," said Fritz.

Faith jumped up and started to run.

"Ow, ow!" she cried.

The ground *was* cold.

The stones *were* sharp.

There *were* stickers in the grass.

"Wait, wait for me," she called.

But the boys were out of sight.

Slowly Faith picked her way back to where her boots lay in the path. Though she set her feet down carefully, watching for stickers and stones, a prickly sticker pierced her toe. A sharp stone bruised her heel.

As she pulled her warm stockings back on her sore feet, Faith's face was wet with crying.

3

Evening

The wind rattled the windows and howled to come in. Faith shivered to hear it. She was sitting on the parlor rug after supper, leaning on Father's knee. The fire in the heater made her cheeks hot. The floor beneath her was cold.

Alena was reading out loud. But Faith wasn't listening. She was thinking about her bad day.

Alena closed the book.

"What a lovely story," she said.

"I think it was sappy," said William.

"Sappy story! Sappy story!" Fritz was laughing.

"That is quite enough," said Mother, laying aside her mending. "It is bedtime for you, Fritz, and you too, Faith."

Faith heard Father's newspaper rustle. She looked up to see his spectacled eyes above the lowered pages.

"Perhaps we might have some apples first?" he said.

"Yes, apples," Faith and her brothers and sister said. "Apples, please, yes!"

"You spoil these children, Father," Mother said.

Father raised his paper. His voice came from behind it. Faith thought it was a smiling voice. "Apples are *good* for children," he said.

"I shall go fetch them," said William importantly.

"Let *me* go, Father," said Fritz.

"May I go?" said Faith, surprising herself. She had never asked before.

Rustle. Rustle. Again Father's newspaper lowered.

Do I *want* to go to the cellar? Faith wondered. It's *dark* down there. But even as she thought it, she was jumping up.

"May I, Father? May I?"

Father looked all around the parlor. He looked at Mother. He looked at Alena. He looked at William and Fritz. But he did not look at Faith.

"Did you hear a little voice offer

to go fetch the apples, Mother?" he said.

"I'll be glad to fetch the apples, Father," said William. "After all, *I'm* the oldest boy."

"William *always* gets to go," said Fritz. "Faith's too young. Send *me* this time."

"Faith?" said Father.

"Yes, me!" yelled Faith, pulling at the edge of his paper until he laid it down. "I'm not too young to go."

"She's only a girl," said Fritz. "She'll be scared."

"I won't be scared," Faith said.

"Why, Faithie," Father said, blinking with pretend surprise. "We were just talking about fetching some apples from the cellar."

"Me, Father. I can fetch them,"

Faith said. "I *won't* be scared."

"How helpful of you to offer," said Father. "Be sure to take a lamp."

"I'll go with you, Faithie, if you like," said Alena.

Faith looked at her big sister's kindly face. Alena was not afraid to go to the cellar. She could hold the lamp high and steady so it lighted all the dark corners. She might hold Faith's hand.

"Yah," said Fritz. "Scaredy Baby Faith needs someone to go with her."

"I can go alone," said Faith. "I won't be scared."

"Yes," said Father. "I think Faith can go alone. Thank you very much, Alena."

But Father wasn't looking at

Alena, Faith saw. He was looking at
Fritz. The look made Fritz hang his
head.

Mother lit a lamp and gave it to
Faith.

"I want a juicy big one," said
Father.

"Take the square-handled basket," Mother said. "Put on your
shawl. Try not to slosh the lamp."

"*I* could do it without all this
fuss," said Fritz.

Faith walked into the hallway,
carefully holding the lamp. She
could hear the wind thumping at
the front door. It gusted under the
door and made her lamp light wa-
ver.

But in the kitchen, the fire, burn-
ing low in the range, made a steady,
rosy glow.

THE CELLAR

I won't be scared, Faith thought. She walked across the kitchen floor by the light from the range and the light from the lamp in her hand. At the back door she tied on her shawl.

It was just a few steps, off the back porch and around the house, to the cellar door. The wind gusted under Faith's skirts. It made her eyes water. It blew her hair.

Faith set down the lamp. She wrestled against the wind to heave open the cellar door.

From out of the dark cellar hole, a whisper of damp touched her face. She felt a prickle at the back of her neck. Her breath caught in her throat.

Faith picked up the lamp and held it before her. She opened her eyes wide to see into the cellar. The light spilled, trembling, down the stairs. Around her the wind cried.

Faith swallowed hard and licked her lips. She groped for the railing. The railing was cold. She felt for the step with her foot.

The basket!

With a rush of relief, Faith remembered the basket. She pulled her foot back. Mother had said, take the square-handled basket.

Faith turned and ran back to the kitchen. She felt the lamp sloshing as she burst through the door.

The square-handled basket was on the table. Slowly she went to get it, taking deep, shaky breaths of warm kitchen air. Her heart slowed down.

Faith put the basket over her arm. Outside, the wind was howling. Inside, the fire murmured softly in the range.

Faith thought that perhaps she would ask Alena to go with her after all. Then she thought how Father trusted her to go by herself. She thought of Fritz's grin.

Faith headed once more for the cellar.

4

Apples

The cellar stairs were narrow and steep. The lamp light threw shadows against the walls. The cold made goose bumps on Faith's arms. Above her the wind whistled over the open door.

One foot after the other, Faith climbed down.

I'm not scared, she kept saying to herself. I'm not scared.

Faith's foot touched the earthen floor of the cellar.

All the way down, she thought. I'm down in the cellar by myself.

Suddenly she knew it was not the wind she was hearing so loud in her ears. It was the sound of her own hard breathing.

Faith held up the lamp to shine on the white stone walls. The walls were lined with shelves of jars.

Jars full of summer, Faith thought. She remembered the summer days when Mother had stood in the kitchen over big, steaming kettles, filling these jars with jams and preserves.

Strawberries, gooseberries, black and red currants. Mulberries, raspberries, yellow and red. Blackcaps

and rhubarb, ground-cherries and peaches. Crab apples, cherries, and plums.

Faith walked along the shelves in the still, cool cellar. The wind was far above her now. She said to herself the sweet summer names. The bright summer colors shone through the glass of the jars.

Faith's cheeks felt hot. Her nose felt cold. It was a good, brave hot and cold. She didn't feel scared.

Pickles. Here were jars of pickles in apple cider vinegar. Cucumber pickles, sour and sweet. Pickled crab apples, peaches, tomatoes. Quarts and quarts of piccalilli and pickled melon rind.

Faith raised her lamp. She peered into the far corner, where the apple barrels stood.

She had to walk around the stacks of pumpkins and squash, cabbages, potatoes, and parsnips in sacks. She had to pass by Mother's cheese press, the one William and Fritz had helped Father to build. Above her, from the rafters, hung the bacon and hams. Their rich, smoky smell made Faith's nose itch.

The light danced on a jar of preserved hens' eggs in slippery water glass. A basket of fresh eggs stood beside it. Sacks of dried sweet corn, dried apples, and peaches. Sorghum and syrup. A jar of white lard. A barrel of vinegar. Bricks of sweet butter. Big wooden barrels of apples!

Faith touched an apple barrel.

Apples! she thought, and I'm *still* not scared.

Carefully she set the lamp on one of the barrels. She put down her basket. She found the barrel with the loosened lid and lifted it off. The barrel was filled with straw. In the straw, like treasure, were the apples.

One by one, Faith counted out an apple each for Father and Mother, for Alena and William and Fritz and her. Big, ripe apples that glowed in the lamplight. One by one, she checked them for soft spots. They were firm and round and cold in her hands.

Her basket was full.

Faith hurried toward the cellar stairs.

Then *bang!* the cellar door fell shut.

She jumped and dropped the lamp. She heard the *pop!* as the hot chimney broke. She smelled the kerosene. The flame snuffed out.

Faith was standing alone in the dark.

She had cried out. The sound still hung in the air. Then there was only quiet and dark and the kerosene smell, strong and bitter in her nose. She opened her mouth. . . .

Then she heard a scuffing at the closed door and the giggle of *Fritz's* voice.

In the middle of what was going to be crying, suddenly Faith stopped.

Fritz had slammed the door! To tease her, as he had been doing all day! He'd made her drop and break the lamp. When she'd come all the way. When she'd come outside and down the steps and clear to the corner and fetched the apples ... and *not been scared!*

Faith tightened her grip on the apple basket. She clenched her teeth and forgot to cry. She felt with her feet to step around the broken lamp and the puddle of kerosene she knew was there. She put out her hand. She groped for a shelf. Then she began to feel her way, panting hard.

A sliver of light appeared. The cellar door was lifting.

"Faith," came Fritz's whisper. He sounded a little scared. "Faithie, you down there?"

Faith did not answer. She

marched toward the sliver of light.

"What happened to your light, Faithie?" Fritz called more loudly down the stairs. "Why's it so dark down there?"

Faith did not answer. She began to climb the stairs.

"Faithie? Father wants to know what's taking so long." Fritz's voice sounded weak and uncertain. "Faithie, *answer* me!"

Faith stomped up the steps, one foot after the other. She could see the light of Fritz's lamp in the crack of the half lifted door.

She pushed against the door with all her might. Fritz jumped back, out of her way. She marched straight past him. She gave him a look with narrowed eyes.

"Faithie!" he shrilled, stumbling

THE CELLAR

beside her around the house and into the kitchen and down the hall. "I didn't mean . . ." His lamp swung wildly as he ran.

The light and the warmth of the parlor reached out to Faith like a hug. She set down the basket with a thump in the doorway.

"I didn't mean anything," Fritz was crying. He rushed past Faith into the parlor. "I'm sorry, Father."

Father looked from Faith to Fritz and back to Faith again.

"Where is your lamp, Faith?" said Mother.

"I dropped it," said Faith, "when the cellar door slammed."

Mother jumped to her feet, hurrying into the hall.

"It didn't catch fire, Mother,"

Faith said. "It just went out. I'm sorry it broke."

Mother stopped, her hand on her heart.

"Merciful heavens!" she said.

"When the door slammed?" said Father, his eyebrows lifting.

"I didn't mean to!" Fritz was crying, his cheeks wet and red.

"I see," said Father. "Fritz, I think you'd best tell your sister you are sorry, while I think what to do about you."

Fritz's lip pushed out. The tears dripped from his chin.

"I'm sorry, Faithie," he said.

Faith looked at Fritz. He looked more scared than she had felt —even when she was going down into the cellar. Even when the door slammed. Even when the lamp went out.

"That's all right," she said to Fritz, surprised that she truly meant it.

"Fritz had better go to bed without an apple tonight," said Father. "Good night, Fritz."

Faith watched Fritz walk slowly from the parlor, hanging his head. The wind was rattling the windows, but Faith scarcely heard it. She was imagining how her apple would taste—sweet and cool and crunchy.

She picked up the basket and carried it to Father.

"There's a big, red, juicy one for you," she told him. "I fetched it by myself!"